# Me at the S

Story by

Pic

Paul Granger and Ruth Owers

A LITTLE LION
Oxford · Batavia · Sydney

I went to the swimming pool for
the first time with Mom and Dad.
I wondered what it would be like.
I changed into a red stripey swimsuit.
I carried a blue stripey towel.

The swimming pool was a beautiful blue.

It looked very very big . . .
. . . and very very wet.

There were lots of other children there learning how to swim. They were laughing and kicking and splashing.

''Swimming is fun,'' said Dad.
''God has given us arms and legs to help us swim.''

I felt a bit frightened and I clung
to Mom.
Dad said, ''Put your toe in the
water — like me.''
And he held me tight.
So I did.

Mom said, ''Put your knees in
next — like me.''
And she held me tight.
So I did.

Dad and Mom said, ''Put your body in next — like us.''

And they both held me tight.
So I did.

I wriggled and splashed and
jumped up and down and
played with Mom and Dad.
IT WAS FUN!

Then Dad said, ''Watch me dive.''
He dived into the water from
a high diving board.
''You'll learn to do that one
day,'' said Mom.
''You'll soon be able
to swim . . .''

''Like a fish . . . or a seal . . .
or a frog . . . or a duck . . .
or a whale . . . or a dog.''

Thank you, God, for water.
Thank you for my arms and legs.
I like learning to swim, God.
Good night.

Published by
**Lion Publishing Corporation**
1705 Hubbard Avenue, Batavia, Illinois 60510, USA
ISBN 0 7459 1734 8

First published 1989



Printed and bound in Yugoslavia